High-Interest/Low-
Trendy Topics: Fiction

14 Reproducible Stories (12-Page Booklets, Each 5.5" x 8.5")
CD Includes: Word for Word Audio Tracks and PDFs of Storybooks and Activities
Featuring 3 Literature Genres: Tales of Adventure, Mysteries, & Scary Stories
and comprehension Activities

A TALE OF ADVENTURE

Bella's Photo

Fiction Story 1

A MYSTERY

The Haunted Classroom

Fiction Story 6

A SCARY STORY

Words on a Wall

Fiction Story 12

by
Jo Browning Wroe
and
Sherrill B. Flora

illustrated by
Julie Anderson

Publisher
Key Education Publishing Company, L.
Minneapolis, Minnesota

CONGRATULATIONS ON YOUR PURCHASE OF A KEY EDUCATION PRODUCT!

The editors at Key Education are former teachers who bring experience, enthusiasm, and quality to each and every product. Thousands of teachers have looked to the staff at Key Education for new and innovative resources to make their work more enjoyable and rewarding. We are committed to developing educational materials that will assist teachers in building a strong and developmentally appropriate curriculum for young children.

PLAN FOR GREAT TEACHING EXPERIENCES WHEN YOU USE EDUCATIONAL MATERIALS FROM KEY EDUCATION PUBLISHING COMPANY, LLC

Credits

Authors: Jo Browning Wroe & Sherrill B. Flora
Inside Illustrations: Julie Anderson
Editors: Claude Chalk & Karen Seberg
Page Design & Layout: Key Education Staff
Cover Design & Production: Annette Hollister-Papp
Audio Voice Talent: Cody Livingood & Sherrill B. Flora

Key Education welcomes manuscripts and product ideas from teachers.
For a copy of our submission guidelines, please send a self-addressed, stamped envelope to:
Key Education Publishing Company, LLC
Acquisitions Department
7309 West 112th Street
Minneapolis, Minnesota 55438

About the Author of the Stories:

Jo Browning Wroe has taught both in the United Kingdom and in the United States. She earned her undergraduate degrees in English and Education from Cambridge University, Cambridge, England. She worked for 12 years in educational publishing before completing a Master's Degree in Creative Writing from the University of East Anglia, Norwich, England. Most of her time is now spent writing teacher resource materials and running workshops for others who love to write. Jo has been the recipient of the National Toy Libraries Award. She lives in Cambridge, England, with her two daughters, Alice and Ruby, and her husband, John.

About the Author of the Activities:

Sherrill B. Flora is the Publisher of Key Education. Sherrill earned her undergraduate degrees in Special Education and Child Psychology from Augustana College and a Master's Degree in Educational Administration from Nova University. Sherrill spent 10 years as a special education teacher in the inner city of Minneapolis before beginning her twenty-year career in educational publishing. Sherrill has authored over 100 teacher resource books, as well as hundreds of other educational games and classroom teaching aids. She has been the recipient of three Directors' Choice Awards, six Parents' Choice Awards, seven Teachers' Choice Awards, and twenty-two Creative Child Magazine Awards. She lives in Minneapolis, Minnesota, with her two daughters, Katie and Kassie, and her very supportive husband, George.

Copyright Notice

Standard Book Number: 978-1-60268-102-6
Trendy Topics: Fiction
Copyright © 2011 by Key Education Publishing Company, LLC
Minneapolis, Minnesota 55438

Contents

How to Make the 14 Storybooks

Each of the fourteen, 12-page, 5.5" x 8.5" storybooks will be made from three 8.5" x 11" sheets of paper. Here is how you copy the reproducible pages and turn the story into a book:

STEP 1: 1st sheet of paper

Copy **cover/page 12** on the front and copy **page 2/page 11** on the back of an 8.5" x 11" sheet of paper. Fold in half.

page 12	cover page 1	page 2	page 11
(front of paper)		*(back of paper)*	

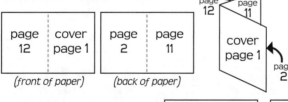

STEP 2: 2nd sheet of paper

Copy **page 10/page 3** on the front and copy **page 4/page 9** on the back of an 8.5" x 11" sheet of paper. Fold in half.

page 10	page 3	page 4	page 9
(front of paper)		*(back of paper)*	

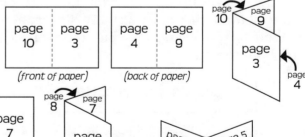

STEP 3: 3rd sheet of paper

Copy **page 8/page 5** on the front and copy **page 6/page 7** on the back of an 8.5" x 11" sheet of paper. Fold in half.

page 8	page 5	page 6	page 7
(front of paper)		*(back of paper)*	

FINAL STEP:

After folding the three sheets of paper, put them together and staple on the fold.

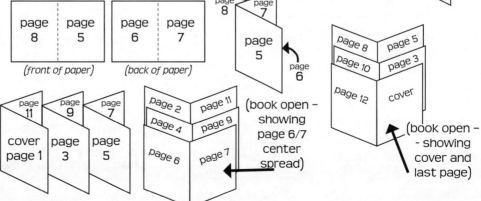

(book open – showing page 6/7 center spread)

(book open – showing cover and last page)

How to Use This Book

Who Is This Book Designed For?

Trendy Topics: Fiction has been written for students who are reading below grade level, for students who have reading disabilities, and for students who are reluctant or discouraged readers.

The Reproducible High-Interest/Low-Readability (and High-Quality) 12-Page Stories

Reading Levels: The engaging stories are written between early-second grade and early-third grade reading levels. Each story's specific reading level can be found below the story title on the **Table of Contents** (page 3). This information will help the teacher choose stories that are appropriate for the individual needs of the students. *(Reading grade levels are not printed on any of the stories or on any of the reproducible activity pages.)*

Design of the Text: The style and size of font and the page layout have been designed to avoid impediments to fluency. Although the text may look the same as in any other book, the spacing between the lines has been increased, the font is larger and easier-to-read, and the ends of the sentences are found most often at the ends of lines in order to facilitate a return sweep. The larger font and simple sentence structure should help children feel more confident as they read.

Illustrations to Increase Text Comprehension: There is one illustration per two-page spread. The student will need to read the text in order to understand the story, yet the illustrations are there to provide picture clues that will help clarify the content.

Vocabulary Instruction

New and Difficult Story Vocabulary: There are new and sometimes difficult vocabulary words that are necessary for the content of each story. Prior to asking a student to read a story, review the story's word list on page 125 and then introduce and practice any unfamiliar words. Make flash cards of the new words and discuss what the words mean. Draw a picture of the word on each card to help students visualize the new vocabulary.

The Read-Along CD

Trendy Topics: Fiction comes with a CD featuring an audio track for each story. The students will hear some music and the title of the story. Then, the story is read on the CD exactly as it is printed on the student's copy of the story.

For many struggling readers, being able to listen to the story first can be extremely beneficial. Knowing the story's content ahead of time provides students with the opportunity to use context clues to help decode words and to interpret the meaning of the story. For other students, being able to track the text as they listen to the words allows for a valuable multisensory experience. Students can hear the words; they can see the words; and they can touch each word as they follow along while listening to the CD.

The Reproducible Activity Pages

Paper and pencil tasks are often "not fun" for struggling readers. There are three activities for each story. The first activity is a full page with many illustrations. The second page is divided into two activities. The teacher may choose to assign both halves of the page at once or cut the page in two and assign each half at different times. The diversity of the activities should encourage the students to finish and not become bored or frustrated.

Coloring, drawing, solving puzzles, and cutting and pasting activities have been included. These types of activities reinforce a wide range of reading skills and are often viewed as "more fun" by the students.

In short, *High-Interest/Low-Readability: Trendy Topics: Fiction* will provide your students with a complete reading experience.

Fill in the blanks. Use the Word Bank.

Word Bank: David   gone   Kenya   photo
picked   small   tents   zebras

1. _____ is Bella's brother.

2. David liked _____ animals.

3. Bella's family went to _____ on a photo safari.

4. It was _____ that Bella wanted to see the most.

5. The family stayed in _____ and camped in Kenya.

6. On the third day, David woke up, and Bella was _____.

7. David _____ up Bella so that the zebras would not run her over.

8. When the family got home, Bella won a _____ contest.

Let's draw a conclusion!

On another sheet of paper, answer this question. What do you think made the "bang" that caused the zebras to run wild?

A TALE OF ADVENTURE

Fiction Story 1

Bella's Photo

When we got home Bella won a photo contest. She won for her photo of the zebras. In the photo, the zebras are running straight at the camera. She had to make a speech when she got the prize.

"I have to thank my brother, David," she said. "If it wasn't for him, there'd be no photo. There'd be no me! Thank you for saving my life.

And, my camera!"

(Page 6)

KE-804090 © Key Education–*Trendy Topics: Adventure – Bella's Photo*

KE-804090 © Key Education–*Trendy Topics: Adventure – Bella's Photo*

(Page 7)

Bella's Photo

"David, Bella, come here! We're going on safari!" Dad yelled to my sister and me. Bella went wild! She loves wildlife and she loves taking photos. This would be her dream vacation.

Not so much for me. I like small animals. I like our cat. I like our hamster. But, big dogs scare me. They bark too loud. They stand too tall. And, horses? Those legs can really kick hard! So, elephants? Giraffes? Zebras? I thought my parents had gone crazy!

I was taller and stronger than Bella. I am her BIG brother! I'm a fullback at school. But still, I was afraid, and she wasn't.

The zebras were running right at Bella. And, she was still taking photos!

I ran towards her. The zebras were running. Their feet sounded like thunder. I ran as fast as I could.

When I got to Bella, I picked her up. Then, I ran fast to get out of the way of the zebras. We fell on the ground. The zebras ran past. We had dust in our eyes and down our throats.

(Page 8)

(Page 9)

"It will help you get over your fear, David," Mom said. "You'll be safe." What Mom said was true. I did feel safe. Kenya was beautiful.

In Kenya, we stayed in camps at night. Each day we went out in a jeep. We saw lions, leopards, and rhinos. Bella had the time of her life. She took hundreds of photos.

"Will we see zebras today?" she asked our guide. It was zebras that Bella wanted to see most.

"Maybe," said the guide.

It wasn't a bad vacation after all. Until the third day . . .

When I woke, Bella was not in her bed. Mom and Dad were asleep.

I went to the door of our tent.

First, I saw the zebras. Then, I saw Bella. Slowly, she was walking over to them. She had her camera around her neck.

There was a loud bang. I still don't know what made that sound. But, it sure scared the zebras. They started to run. Their hooves made so much dust. It looked like a dust storm.

(Page 10)

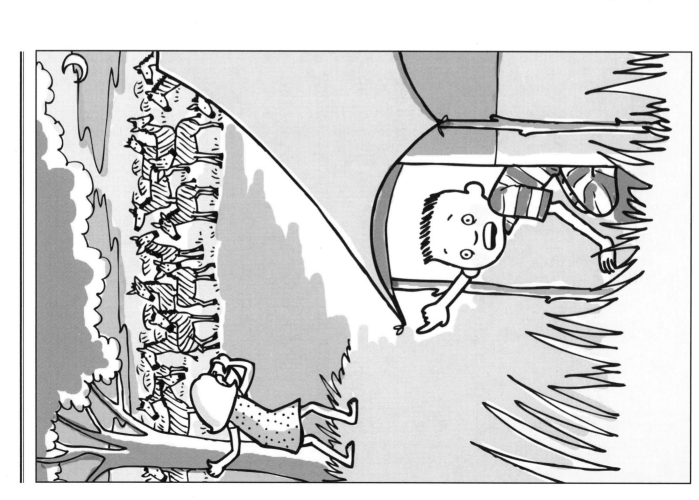

Name

Directions: Read the words in the boxes at the bottom of the page. Which words describe Bella? Which words describe David? Which words describe both of them? Cut out the word boxes along the dotted lines and glue them into the correct sections of the Venn diagram.

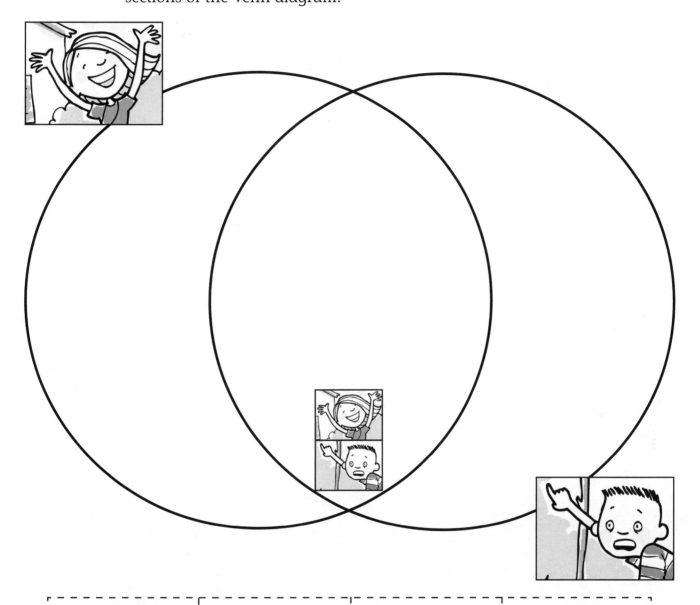

won a photo contest	likes small animals	loves taking photos	rode in a jeep
saved them from the zebras	plays football	went on safari	loves wildlife

Name

Directions: Circle the words from the Word Bank in the word search.
The words may be horizontal or vertical.

Word Bank

Bella
David
elephants
jeep
Kenya
lion
photos
safari
tents
wild
zebras

e	l	e	p	h	a	n	t	s
b	n	t	h	o	n	z	y	a
t	K	h	o	j	e	e	p	f
t	e	n	t	s	l	b	n	a
u	n	r	o	e	i	r	l	r
c	y	s	s	e	o	a	o	i
D	a	v	i	d	n	s	v	j
w	i	l	d	B	e	l	l	a

Directions: Read each sentence about the story. Write a "**T**" on the blank if the sentence is true. Write an "**F**" on the blank if the sentence is false.

1. Bella and David went to Kenya. _____

2. At first, David did not want to go. _____

3. The family stayed at a nice hotel. _____

4. A herd of zebras almost ran over David and Bella. _____

5. The family saw lots of monkeys eating bananas. _____

6. When the family got home, Bella won a photo contest. _____

Fill in the blanks. Use the Word Bank.

Word Bank:　beach　camels　carpet　flower
magic　men　room　sit　smell　stone

1. Tom loves the _____ in the store window.

2. Mike does not like things that _____ musty and dusty.

3. Tom says that the carpet is _____.

4. Tom says that to make the magic carpet fly, you must _____ on it and rub the blue _____.

5. Mike sits on the carpet and the _____ begins to spin.

6. Mike lands on the _____ and sees _____.

7. Two _____ run past Mike.

8. One man trips, and a blue _____ flies out of his hand.

Let's draw a conclusion!

On another sheet of paper, answer these questions: When Mike returned, he still had the blue stone. What is the blue stone? Why did those men want tit?

(Page 13)

A TALE OF ADVENTURE

THE FLYING CARPET

Fiction Story 2

Suddenly, I hear, "Mike, get up! It's time to go."

I look up at Tom. My face is on the carpet.

"Did you have fun?" Tom asks.

I tell him that I fell asleep.

"That's what you think," says Tom.

Then, I stand up. "There's no such thing as a magic carpet."

"Then, how did you get that?" Tom asks.

"Get what?" I ask.

"That," and Tom points to my hand.

I look and am so surprised. A blue stone is in my hand.

"Come home with me," says Tom. "I'll show you all the stuff I've come back with. We're going to have so many great adventures!"

(Page 14)

(Page 15)

THE FLYING CARPET

"Mike, see that carpet?" asks my friend Tom. We are looking in a store window. We pass this store every day. It sells old stuff—lamps, sofas, tables, and carpets. Tom loves going in this store! I don't. It's dusty and musty. I don't like the smell. I like things that smell new. But, there is a carpet inside that Tom loves.

"What's so special about the carpet?" I ask. "I'm hungry, and I want to go home."

There are two men running along the beach. One man is chasing the other man. They are close to me now.

"Stop, thief!" shouts one of the men.

"I'm no thief. It's my stone. You'll never get it," yells the other man.

They both run past me. The man in front trips. He falls in the water. A blue stone flies out of his hand. The other man falls on top of the first.

And, I catch the stone.

(Page 16)

(Page 17)

"It's magic," he says.

"Yeah, right," I say. I look at it. It's blue and red and old and shabby.

Tom says to me, "It's true. That carpet has taken me on rides."

"Yeah, right," I say, again.

"Come in with me—you'll see," says Tom.

"No way. I'm going home."

But Tom begs, "It won't take long. I'll talk to the guy at the back of the store. I'll make sure he doesn't see you. You just go sit on the carpet. Then, rub the blue flower three times."

So, I sit on the carpet. It feels softer than it looks. I see the blue flower. I rub it once. Twice. Three times.

Nothing.

I'm so mad at Tom.   And, I feel stupid.

I call for him, but my voice is weird.

The room starts to spin.   I'm going up.

I can feel air. The air is warm.

There is water below me. It's the sea.

I'm not scared. I feel safe. I feel free.

Finally, the carpet lands. I'm on a
beach. There are camels, and it's so hot!
The sand burns my feet. I walk down to
the water.

KE-804090 © Key Education–*Trendy Topics: Adventure – The Flying Carpet*

(Page 18)

KE-804090 © Key Education–*Trendy Topics: Adventure – The Flying Carpet*

Name _____

Directions: This is the store that has the flying carpet. Follow the directions.

FOLLOW THE DIRECTIONS

1. Find the flying carpet and draw a flower on it.

2. Color the carpet yellow, and then color the flower on the carpet blue.

3. Color Mike's shirt red.

4. Color Tom's shirt blue.

5. Color the horse and the treasure chest brown.

6. Color one lamp green and the other lamp orange.

7. Think of a name for the store. Then, print it in the space above the window.

Cause and Effect

Directions: A **cause** tells why something has happened and an **effect** tells what happened. Draw a line from each cause in **Column A** to its matching effect in **Column B**.

Column A

1. Sit on the carpet and rub the blue flower three times,

2. Walking on the hot sand

3. A man running on the beach trips

4. A stone flies out of the running man's hand,

Column B

a. burned Mike's feet.

b. and Mike catches it.

c. and the rug will fly.

d. and falls in the water.

Directions: Make a list of the places that you would want to visit on a flying carpet.

Creative Writing

1.
2.
3.
4.
5.
6.
7.
8.
9.
10.

Fill in the blanks. Use the Word Bank.

Word Bank:

arrested	baby	black	bottle
glass	grab	message	police	read	sleep

1. At the beach, Hilary's parents _____ and _____ books.

2. The baby picked up a _____ bottle.

3. Hilary took the glass _____ from the _____ .

4. Then, a man with _____ sunglasses was staring at Hilary.

5. Hilary saw there was a _____ in the bottle.

6. The man tried to _____ the bottle from Hilary.

7. Hilary ran and bumped into a _____ officer.

8. The police officer called for backup and the man was _____ .

Let's draw a conclusion!

On another sheet of paper, describe the message. Do you think the person that wrote the message was ever arrested?

(Page 21)

A TALE OF ADVENTURE

Fiction Story 3

"I know him," the officer said. "He's bad news. He robs houses."

"Why does he want this bottle?" I asked.

The police officer smashed it. He read the paper. "It's an address. It's telling him which house to rob next."

We looked at the man. He was walking away. The officer called for backup. And then, the ugly thief was arrested!

"Where are your parents?" the officer said.

I took him to them. They had just woken up.

"Good day. I'm Officer James. Your daughter has just stopped a thief."

Dad looked at Mom and asked, "Am I awake, or is this a dream?"

(Page 22)

(Page 23)

Message in a Bottle

I'm Hilary, and I'm the only kid in my family.

It's OK most of the time. Just one time a year I wish I wasn't. In July, when we go to the beach. When I was small, Mom and Dad played with me. Now, they sleep and read books. I just sit and watch the other kids play. Some do. Some don't.

I hope they ask me to join in. Some do. Some don't.

Last year, no one asked. But, I don't mind. Now, I'm a hero because I was on my own.

"Hey, kid!" It was the big ugly man.

"What?" I answered.

"That's my bottle!" he growled.

Bravely, I said, "Who says? I found it."

He tried to grab it. He was stronger, but I was faster. I ran back towards Mom and Dad. Then, bump!

"Easy, kid!" It was a police officer.

"Sorry," I said. I turned around. The ugly man was looking at the sea. He looked like he didn't care about me or the bottle.

I gave the police officer the bottle.

"I found this in the sea. That man is chasing me. He wants it."

"What man?" asked the police officer.

"Him," I pointed.

KE-804090 © Key Education–Trendy Topics: Adventure – Message in a Bottle

(Page 24)

KE-804090 © Key Education–Trendy Topics: Adventure – Message in a Bottle

(Page 25)

The beach was full of people. A baby sat on the sand. His family was playing on the beach. The baby picked up a glass bottle. I got up. I took the bottle from the baby.

"What are you doing?" asked his mom.

"Your baby had a glass bottle," I said.

"Oh! Thank you," she smiled at me.

I sat down with the bottle. My mom and dad were asleep. I saw a big man a few feet away. Was he staring at me? He was ugly. He wore black sunglasses.

I stood the bottle in the sand and laid down. Then, I saw it! A piece of paper was in the bottle. A message! I tipped the bottle over. The paper didn't come out. My mom and dad were still asleep. I got up and walked. I needed a twig to get the paper out.

(Page 26)

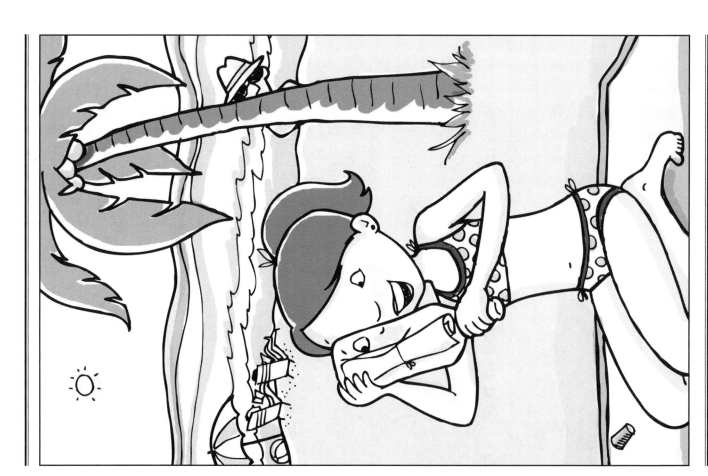

Name _____

Sequence

Directions: Look at the pictures at the bottom of the page.
Cut them out along the dotted lines and glue them in the correct order.

1	2	3

Draw a picture of Hilary.	Write a sentence about Hilary.
Draw a picture of the thief.	Write a sentence about the thief.

Directions: Circle **yes** or **no** for each sentence.

Drawing Conclusions

1. Hilary is the only child in her family.   **yes**   **no**

2. The baby was playing with matches.   **yes**   **no**

3. A man wearing sunglasses tried to grab the
   bottle from Hilary.   **yes**   **no**

4. Hilary gave the man wearing sunglasses the bottle.   **yes**   **no**

5. The message in the bottle said, "Come to my house."   **yes**   **no**

6. The thief was never arrested.   **yes**   **no**

7. Hilary's dad asked, "Am I awake or is this a dream?"   **yes**   **no**

Fill in the blanks. Use the Word Bank.

Word Bank: bear   crashed   fast   good   growl   Marc   not   Slow   snow   stop

1. Jon wanted _____ to go skiing with him.

2. Marc was _____ a good skier.

3. Marc's dad was a very _____ skier.

4. When Marc went skiing with his dad he said,

5. Marc heard a _____ and saw a

6. Marc skied _____ to get away from the bear.

7. Marc's dad saw him and yelled,
   " _____ down!"

8. Marc _____ into his dad and fell into a heap on the _____.

" I can't _____ . "

Let's draw a conclusion!

On another sheet of paper, answer this question. It was winter, and bears usually hibernate. Why do you think this bear was awake?

(Page 29)

A TALE OF ADVENTURE

Fiction Story 4

NEVER AGAIN!

CRASH!

"Dad and I fell into a heap on the snow."

"You were fast!" Dad got up.
"You told me you couldn't ski!"

"I didn't say that!" I said. "I told you I couldn't stop."

Dad rubbed his bumped head. "I can teach you that part," he said. "When did you learn how to ski so fast?"

"Today," I said, "with a little help from a bear."

(Page 30)

(Page 31)

NEVER AGAIN!

My friend Jon asked me to go away with him.

"Where to?" I asked.

"To ski in the mountains," Jon said.

I said, "Thanks, but no thanks."

"Why not, Marc?" asked Jon.

So, I told him, "I went once. Never again will I go skiing! You see, my dad is a great skier. I'm not. It was our last day. He wanted me to go on the steep slope with him."

"Then what did you do?" asked Jon.

"There was only one thing to do. I felt the skis under my feet. I held the poles in my hand. I looked at the steep white slope in front of me. And, I pushed off."

"I didn't look back. I went faster and faster. I didn't know how to stop at the bottom. I didn't care. I had to get away from that bear."

Dad was at the bottom of the slope. "Slow down!" he yelled.

"I can't!" I yelled back.

(Page 32)

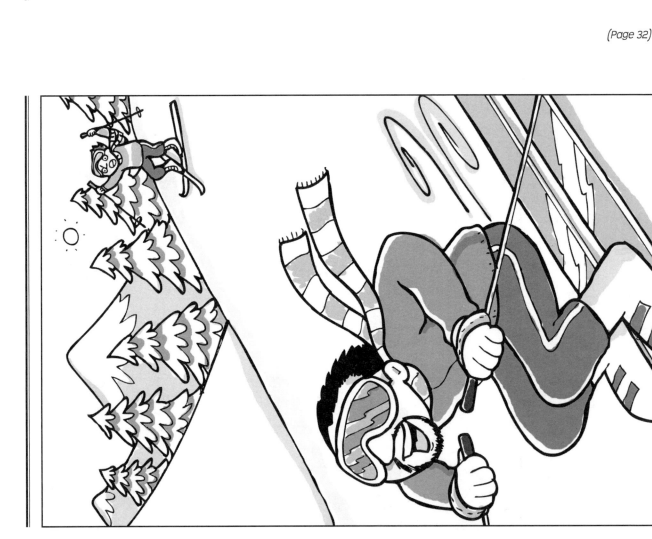

(Page 33)

When we got to the top, I didn't want to come down.

"I can't stop. I can't slow down," I said.

"Oh, you'll be fine," my dad said. And, away he went—and fast!

"Dad, wait!" I yelled, "but he went down the slope. I heard him laugh as he skied away."

Jon said to me, "You must have been scared."

"Yeah," I said. "But, that was just the start."

Surprised, Jon asked, "There's more?"

"Much more! I stopped by some trees. I was too scared to go down. I was too scared to stay up. Then, I saw a flash of brown to my left. I heard a deep growl. My legs turned to jello. It was a bear. Three feet away from me was a huge, brown bear!"

"What did you do?" asked Jon.

"Well, I looked at that bear. And, the bear looked at me. He tossed his head and growled—at me!"

(Page 34)

Name _____

Directions: Read the sentences at the bottom of the page.
Cut out each sentence and glue it under its matching picture.

1.

(glue here)

2.

(glue here)

3.

(glue here)

4.

(glue here)

Dad and I fell into a heap at the bottom of the hill.	"Hey, would you like to go skiing with me?"
I saw a bear, and it growled at me!	My dad is a great skier!

Name _____

Directions: Read the question in each box. Write your answer in each thought bubble.

1. What do you think the boy is thinking?

2. What do you think the dad is thinking?

Main Idea

Directions: The **main idea** tells what the story is about. Read the following sentences and circle the sentence that you think best explains the main idea of the story.

1. Bears chase people who like to ski.

2. One bad ski experience and I will never ski again!

3. My father is the best skier!

Fill in the blanks. Use the Word Bank.

Word Bank: Cal   cold   crack   help   help
ice   man   Paul   skate   sled   snow

1. _____ once lived in Michigan.

2. Cal loved the _____ and _____.

3. Cal wanted to _____ on the lake.

4. _____ shook his head and walked away.

5. Max could hear the ice _____.

6. Cal was in the _____ water.

7. Max yelled, "_____!" Someone

8. A _____ pulled Cal to safety on a _____.

Let's draw a conclusion!

On another sheet of paper, answer this question. Pretend you are Cal's parent. You just found out what he did. What would you say to him?

(Page 37)

A TALE OF ADVENTURE

On Thin Ice

Fiction story 5

"Cal! Cal!" It was Paul and Max. I opened my eyes. I saw lights. I saw people.

"Hang on, Cal. They'll come and get you."

There was a man on a sled. I started to cry. He pulled me onto the sled.

"You're lucky. You have good friends."

Paul and Max hugged me.

"I'm sorry," I said. "Thanks for getting help."

"Don't ever do that again," Max said.

"Don't worry, I won't," I said.

KE-804090 © Key Education –Trendy Topics: Adventure - On Thin Ice

(Page 38)

KE-804090 © Key Education –Trendy Topics: Adventure - On Thin Ice

(Page 39)

On Thin Ice

I grew up in Michigan. Winters there were long and hard. But, I loved the snow! When we moved to Texas, I missed the snow and ice.

During my third winter in Texas, it snowed! We rode sleds. We had snowball fights. We built snowmen. We built snowwomen. We built snow dogs and snow cats. But, I wanted more. I wanted to skate on a lake again. My friends didn't.

"It's not safe, Cal," Max said to me.

"You're wimps," I said. "In Michigan, we always skated on the lakes."

"Get help!" I yelled to Max.

"I don't want to leave you!" He was so upset.

"Go! Get help."

Max ran away. I could hear him shout, "Help! Someone help!"

I was afraid to move. My leg felt dead. I laid on the ice. I closed my eyes. I wanted to sleep. I knew I should stay awake, but it was hard—so hard.

(Page 40)

-8-

(Page 41)

"The ice isn't very thick," said Paul.

"I'm not going."

"OK," I said, "Have fun sitting and watching TV!"

"Are you really going to do this?" Paul asked.

"You bet," I said.

Paul just shook his head. Then, he walked away.

So, I turned to Max and asked, "You'll come, won't you?"

-5-

I was so mad. I wanted Max to come, too. It was no fun to skate on the lake alone. I stepped onto the ice. It sank a little under my feet. I had to keep going. Max would think I was afraid.

Max yelled at me. "Cal, come back. I can hear the ice cracking!"

"Are you all babies here?" I tried to sound brave. I knew I should have turned back. But, I was dumb! I walked out to the middle of the lake.

There was a crack. My left foot sank in the water. It was so cold. I saw the look on Max's face. He was so scared.

The water was up to my knees. My leg was numb. If more ice cracked, I'd fall in.

(Page 42)

Directions: Read the question in each box. Write your answer in each speech bubble.

1. What do you think Max is thinking?

2. What do you think Max is yelling?

3. What do you think Cal is thinking?

4. What do you think Cal is thinking now?

Directions: Pretend you are a reporter for the newspaper.
What two questions would you ask Cal?

1.

2.

Directions: A **cause** tells why something has happened and an **effect** tells what
happened. Draw a line from each cause in **Column A** to its matching
effect in **Column B**.

Column A

Column B

1. In Michigan, winters were long
   and hard,

2. Cal stepped onto the lake and

3. More ice cracked and

4. Max ran for help

a. Cal fell into the water.

b. and found a man with a sled
   who could pull Cal out of the
   water.

c. and Cal could skate on the
   frozen lakes.

d. heard the ice crack.

Fill in the blanks. Use the Word Bank.

Word Bank: book   eating   field   ghost   money
mouse   Mrs. Green   Toby   walked   washed   zoo

1. Toby's class was going on a _____

   trip to the _____.

2. _____

3. Toby had to earn _____ for the

   field trip.

4. Toby _____ had never been to the zoo.

5. One day, _____ was upset.

6. Someone had ripped up a _____

   in Mrs. Green's closet.

7. Maybe a _____ was in the closet.

8. Toby saw that a _____ was

   _____ the books.

Let's draw a conclusion!

On another sheet of paper, answer this question.
Mrs. Green said they should catch the mouse
and take it to the zoo. How do you think they
should catch it?

(Page 45)

A MYSTERY

Fiction Story 6

I saw no one. A book was on the floor. It was all torn. Then, I saw it. There! A tiny brown body. It ran along the shelf. A mouse! A mouse was eating our books!

I told Mrs. Green.

She said, "Perhaps we should catch it. Then, we could take it to the zoo with us!"

(Page 46)

(Page 47)

The Haunted Classroom

Our school is in a big city. Some kids at school are rich. Lots of kids are not rich. I'm not rich.

My mom is not well. She can't get out of the house much.

When my teacher, Mrs. Green, told us about the school field trip, my heart sank. It was going to be a great trip. We were going to the zoo. I had never been to the zoo.

Mrs. Green saw that I was upset. She knew why. She talked to me after school. "Toby, do some jobs. Earn some money for the trip."

I had to find out who was hurting the books! After school, I hid in the bathroom. When Mrs. Green left, I snuck back into the classroom. I waited. I waited a long time. Would anyone come?

Then, I heard it. Something in the closet hit the floor. But, there was no one in the closet. It had to be a ghost!

I wanted to run. But, I wanted to go to the zoo even more! I had to open the closet door. My heart pounded. I pulled open the door.

(Page 48)

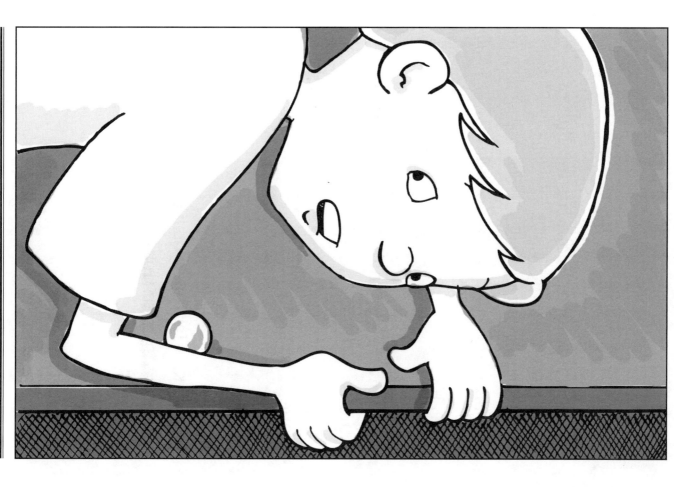

(Page 49)

So, I did. I washed cars. I walked dogs. I babysat. Soon, I had the money, and I was so happy. The trip to the zoo was in three days.

The next day at school something was wrong. Mrs. Green always had a smile for us. But, not this morning—she looked upset.

"Someone has been in my closet. They've ripped up a book. This is not funny. Who was it?"

No one spoke. I looked around. Everyone looked at everyone else.

"I will find out," said Mrs. Green.

The next morning, Mrs. Green was still not smiling.

She held up a book. The top half of the book was missing.

She asked again, "Who did this?"

Silence.

"Often," she said, "I can tell who is guilty. I can feel it, but not this time. Unless the closet has a ghost, it has to be one of you."

Silence.

"OK." Her face was like stone. "If no one owns up to this, the zoo trip is off."

"No!" I yelled, "That's not fair."

"Life is not fair," she said.

(Page 50)

Visual Discrimination

Directions: This is Mrs. Green's closet. Maybe there was more than one mouse.
Can you find all of the mice in Mrs. Green's closet? Color all of the mice.

Name _____

Directions: Read each question.
Circle the picture that answers each question.

1. Where was Mrs. Green's class going on a field trip?

2. What did Toby take on walks to earn money?

3. What did Toby wash to earn money?

4. What was eating the books?

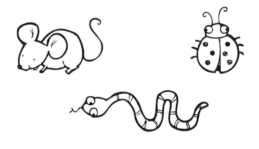

Directions: Make a list of all of the things that you could do to earn money for a field trip.

1. _____
2. _____
3. _____
4. _____
5. _____

6. _____
7. _____
8. _____
9. _____
10. _____

Fill in the blanks. Use the Word Bank.

Word Bank: birthday give grandma loved never pillow ring slipper table tiptoed water

1. Aunt Sue was more like a _____.

2. Mary _____ Aunt Sue's ruby _____.

3. One night, Mary found the ruby ring on her _____.

4. Mary _____ into Aunt Sue's room and put the ring on the _____.

5. Next, the ring was in Mary's _____.

6. Then, the ring was in the _____ glass.

7. Mary would _____ take Aunt Sue's ring!

8. Aunt Sue will _____ Mary the ring on her 18th _____.

Let's draw a conclusion!

On another sheet of paper, write a story about why you think the ruby ring is so important to Aunt Sue.

(Page 53)

A MYSTERY

Fiction Story 7

"Oh, yes, I will." Aunt Sue was standing at the door.

"Sue, what is going on?" asked Mom.

"I love this ring very much. But, I am getting old. I want my ring to have a good home. I want someone to have it whom I can trust.

She looked at the ring on her finger. Then, she looked at me. "I put it in your room each night as a test. And, you did the right thing. Each night, you gave it back to me. When you are eighteen, this ring will be yours. Until then, it stays on my finger."

Tomorrow is my birthday. At last, I'm going to be eighteen.

(Page 54)

KE-804090 © Key Education–*Trendy Topics: Mystery – The Ring*

KE-804090 © Key Education–*Trendy Topics: Mystery – The Ring*

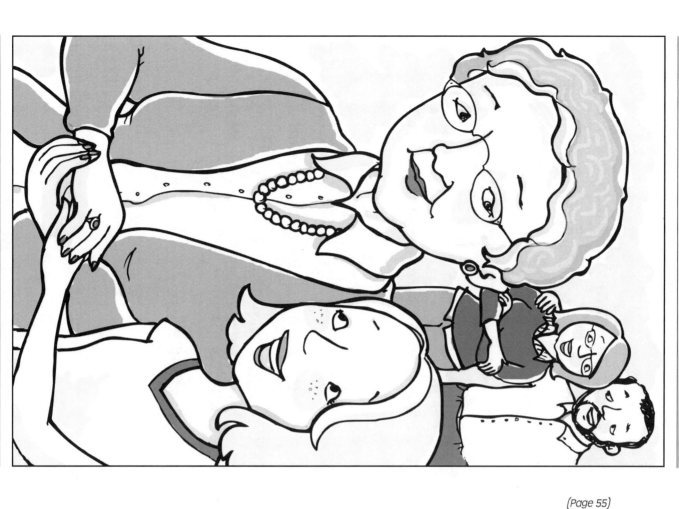

(Page 55)

The Ring

Aunt Sue is Dad's sister. She used to come and stay with us for a week every April. Aunt Sue was older than my dad. She looked more like a grandma.

She didn't like a lot of noise. She was very neat and tidy. Her clothes were like an old lady's. But, there was one thing I loved about Aunt Sue. I loved her ruby ring.

Aunt Sue never took off the ring. It sparkled red. It was the most beautiful thing I had ever seen. Every year, I asked if I could try it on.

She'd say, "No, Mary! This ring never comes off my finger."

Mom found me in tears. I told her

about the ring. "I find it in the middle

of the night. Then, I have to sneak into

Aunt Sue's room and put it back!"

Mom said, "Maybe you take it when

you are asleep."

"No, Mom! It's not me! I would

never just take Aunt Sue's ring.

If you don't believe me, Aunt Sue really

won't believe me."

(Page 56)

(Page 57)

When I was twelve, the ring did come off her finger. Things were never the same again.

When Aunt Sue came to visit, she would sleep in my room. I would sleep in my brother's room. I didn't sleep very well in there. I often woke up in the night.

One night that year, I woke up and saw something on my pillow. It sparkled red. It was Aunt Sue's ring! How did it get there? I had to take it back! I tiptoed into her room. I put it on the table.

The next night, I woke up again.

I needed a drink. I went to the kitchen.

When I went back to bed, there it was again — in my slipper! The ring was in my slipper!

I had to put it back again. I tiptoed into Aunt Sue's room. I was shaking.

I put the ring on her table.

On the third night, I didn't wake up.

But, in the morning, there it was AGAIN.

This time it was in my water glass.

It was too late to take it back!

KE-804090 © Key Education–Trendy Topics: Mystery – The Ring

(Page 58)

KE-804090 © Key Education–Trendy Topics: Mystery – The Ring

Name _____

Directions: Choose a word from the Word Bank to answer each crossword question. Write the answer in the correct word boxes.

Word Bank

Aunt Sue   Mary   ring   ruby   sleep   sparkle

ACROSS	**DOWN**
4. Mary loved Aunt Sue's ruby _____.	1. The ruby ring would _____.
5. The ring had a large _____ stone in it.	2. _____ did not take the ruby ring.
6. When Mary went to _____ the ring would appear in her room.	3. Mary worried that _____ would think she took the ring.

Name _____

Directions: Design a ring that you would like to wear.

Directions: Read each sentence about the story. Write a "**T**" on the blank if the sentence is true. Write an "**F**" on the blank if the sentence is false.

1.   Aunt Sue would visit every April and stay for a week. _____

2.   Mary thought Aunt Sue's ring was beautiful. _____

3.   Aunt Sue dressed like a teenager. _____

4.   Aunt Sue only wore her ring during the day. _____

5.   Mary found Aunt Sue's ring on her pillow. _____

6.   Aunt Sue will give Mary the ring on Mary's 18th birthday. _____

Fill in the blanks. Use the Word Bank.

Word Bank: aunt friends ghost Lady Lake
quiet sandbar sit walk white

1. Every summer the kids would see the _____ of the _____.

2. The uncle said to _____ and be _____.

3. The Lady of the Lake wore a _____ dress.

4. The Lady of the Lake could _____ on water.

5. The little boy thought the Lady of the Lake was a _____!

6. When the boy was 18, he brought his _____ to the lake.

7. The boys found a large _____.

8. The boy's _____ was the Lady of the Lake.

Let's draw a conclusion!

On another sheet of paper, answer this question. How do you think the aunt changed clothes, went to the lake, and got into the water without being seen?

(Page 61)

A MYSTERY

Fiction Story 8

The Lady of the Lake

"I know why they didn't let you swim this far." Phil rose up. He was standing on the water!

"Come on up," Phil laughed.

I swam towards him. "Ouch!" My hand hit something hard. So did my feet.

Under the water was a huge sandbar. I climbed up on it and stood next to Phil.

"This is why my aunt was never there," I said. "She was the Lady of the Lake!"

(Page 62)

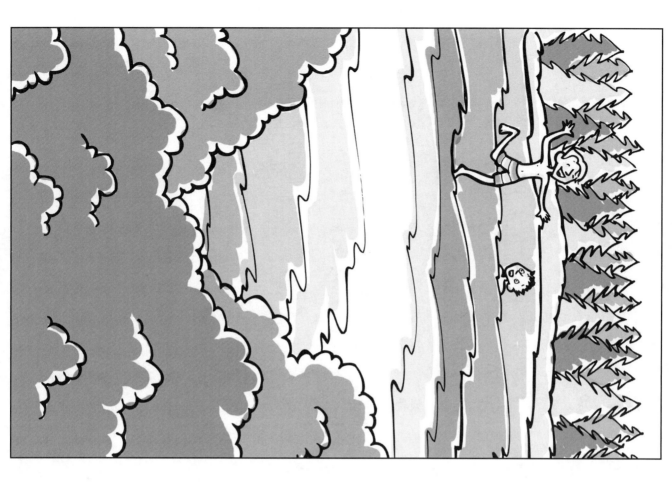

(Page 63)

The Lady of the Lake

My cousins had the best cabin. It was on the shore of a lake — a haunted lake. I went there for two weeks every summer. On my first night, we always saw the Lady of the Lake. My uncle, my cousins, and I would go and look for the Lady of the Lake. My aunt stayed in the cabin. She was scared of the Lady of the Lake.

Every year it was the same. They would meet me at the bus. We would drive to the cabin and eat dinner outside. Then, we would go for a walk by the lake.

"Do you think she'll come?" I'd ask.

"Let's hope she does," one of my cousins would say.

The next morning Phil and I went for a swim.

"I feel like an idiot," I said as we swam out. "But, I did see her. I saw her every year."

We kept swimming. "I've never been out this far. They never let me swim out this far when I was a kid."

"Ouch!" Phil was ahead of me.

"What's up?" I said.

"Was this where the ghost was?" Phil asked.

I looked back to the shore. "I guess so."

(Page 64)

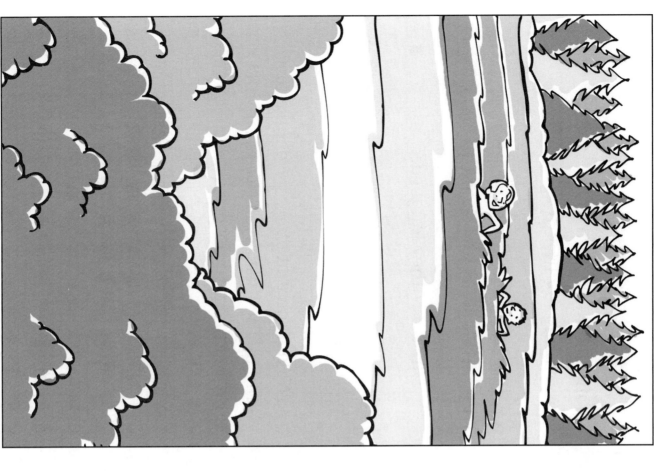

(Page 65)

"We have to sit still and be quiet," my uncle would say. I was scared and happy all at the same time.

I always saw her first. "Look! Look!" I'd shout.

Far away, a woman would come out of the water. She would stand and stare at us. She wore a long white dress. She had to be a ghost. She could walk on water!

I went back there when I was eighteen. My aunt and uncle said I could bring my friends.

"My aunt and uncle live by a haunted lake," I told them.

"Sure it is!" they laughed.

"You wait," I said. "You'll see her— 'The Lady of the Lake.'"

We got there at dusk. "We have to stand by the lake. We have to sit still and be quiet," I said.

We sat there for an hour. The stars came out. The sky turned black. She didn't show. I felt stupid. My friends didn't seem to mind. They liked the cabin and the lake.

(Page 66)

Directions: Make up your own story about the Lady of the Lake.

Directions: Read each question. Circle the correct answer.

1. Where was the cabin?

| by a large river | in the north woods | on the shore of a lake |

_____

2. What did the kids have to do to see the Lady of the Lake?

| sing a song | cover their eyes | sit and be quiet |

_____

3. Who was the Lady of the Lake?

| a neighbor | a ghost | the aunt |

Draw a picture of the young boy.	Write a sentence about him.
Draw a picture of "The Lady of the Lake."	Write a sentence about her.

Fill in the blanks. Use the Word Bank.

Word Bank: blue   buy   doctor   jeans   legs   liked
mayo   pickles   popsicles   sick   week

1. Luke _____ going to see the _____ .

2. Luke got _____ from the doctor.

3. Luke got sick and his _____ turned _____ .

4. The dye from Luke's _____ made his legs blue.

5. Everyday for a _____ Luke threwup.

6. Luke made his pretend "throw-up" with _____ and _____ .

7. Luke pretended to be _____ just to get popsicles.

8. Luke's mom said that she would _____ him some popsicles.

Let's draw a conclusion!

On another sheet of paper, answer this question. What do you think about what Luke did?

KE-804090 © Key Education–Trendy Topics: Mystery – Sick Brother

(Page 69)

A MYSTERY

Sick Brother

Fiction Story 9

"What are you saying?" Dad asked.

"Luke made it. It's not real," said the doctor.

Luke shook his head. A teardrop fell down his cheek.

"Are you unhappy at school, Luke?" asked Mom.

"No," Luke said.

"Then, why?" asked Dad. "Why did you do this? You have to tell us."

"I like the doctor's popsicles." Luke's voice was soft.

"But, Luke," Mom said, "you can have popsicles at home."

"I can?" He looked up at Mom. "But, we never have any popsicles."

"We can buy some," said Dad.

Luke grinned, then said, "let's go shopping!"

(Page 70)

KE-804090 © Key Education–*Trendy Topics: Mystery – Sick Brother*

KE-804090 © Key Education–*Trendy Topics: Mystery – Sick Brother*

(Page 71)

Sick Brother

My little brother, Luke, was cute. He had blonde hair and big brown eyes. He had a funny grin.

The year Luke started school, he got sick. His teacher was worried. My parents were worried. I was even worried.

First, his legs turned blue. Not bright blue, just a hint of blue.

"Maybe it's his blood," Mom said.

"We should take him to the doctor," Dad said.

The next day my mom called the doctor. He said he would like to see Luke.

When we got to the doctor's office, my mom asked, "Is it bad, Doctor?"

"I think we know why his legs are blue," the doctor said. "Does Luke have new blue jeans?"

"Yes. He got them last week!" said Mom.

Then, the doctor said, "I think it's the dye from his jeans. That's what turned his legs blue."

The doctor smiled at Luke. Luke was quiet. He looked down at the floor.

"And, Luke threw up pickles and mayo." The doctor looked at Luke. Then, he looked at Mom and Dad. "But, that was not from Luke's tummy. Or, even from his mouth."

Mom looked at Luke. Luke was trying not to cry.

(Page 72)

(Page 73)

My brother liked going to see the doctor. He liked the popsicles the doctor gave him.

The doctor looked in Luke's mouth. He looked in his eyes and his ears.

"I can't see anything wrong. Keep an eye on him," he said.

Then, the doctor asked Luke if he would like a popsicle.

"Yes, please," said my brother.

The next day Luke threw up.
He threw up every day for a week.

My parents were really worried.
What if he was really sick?

They called the doctor again.
And again he said to bring him in.
He still didn't know what was wrong with Luke.

The doctor said, "Next time he throws up, bring some of 'it' to me. We can run tests on it."

"Yuck!" I said.

"If it helps your brother, we must do it," said Mom.

So, she did. She took my brother's puke to the doctor.

(Page 74)

Name

Directions: Look at the pictures. Write a sentence about what you think is happening next to each picture.

Name

Directions: Read the question in each box. Write your answer in each speech bubble.

| 1. What do you think Luke is thinking? | 2. What do you think Luke is saying? |

Fact or Opinion

Directions: A **fact** is something that is true. An **opinion** is something that a person thinks, believes, or feels. Write the word "**fact**" or the word "**opinion**" next to each sentence.

_____ 1. Luke's legs turned blue.

_____ 2. Luke should go to see the doctor.

_____ 3. Luke likes popsicles!

_____ 4. Luke's parents were really worried.

_____ 5. Pickles and mayo are yucky.

_____ 6. Luke was not sick.

Fill in the blanks. Use the Word Bank.

Word Bank: Animal   back   black   bite
dog   dream   hitting   Homer   long   smelled

1. The boy and his dad went to _____

    Rescue to get a _____.

2. The dog was named _____.

3. Homer's fur was _____ and

    _____.

4. Homer was the boy's _____ dog.

5. Homer tried to _____ the boy's dad.

6. The dad wanted to take Homer _____

    _____ to Animal Rescue.

7. At Animal Rescue, they heard a mean man

    _____ a dog.

8. The mean man and the dad's aftershave

    _____ the same.

Let's draw a conclusion!

On another sheet of paper, answer this question. Homer is the boy's "dream dog." What would your "dream dog" be like?

(Page 77)

A MYSTERY

Fiction Story 10

"Dad, we have to talk!" I pulled him out of the room. "It's the aftershave."

"You smell like that man. Homer's scared of you! You don't wear it on the weekends. Homer was fine both weekends."

Dad looked at Homer in the car. He saw us. He wagged his tail.

"I hope you're right, son."

We took Homer home. Dad threw away the aftershave. He called Animal Rescue. Homer and Dad have been friends ever since.

(Page 78)

(Page 79)

HOMER

I'd always wanted a dog. I begged my dad every day, twice a day.

"OK, OK," he finally said. "On your next birthday, you can get a dog."

I hugged him. I ran all around the house. I cheered I was so happy. My next birthday was tomorrow.

Dad said, "Tomorrow, we'll go to Animal Rescue. You can pick out a dog."

I chose the biggest dog. I named him Homer. Homer's fur was long and black. His nose was soft.

That weekend, we went to the park. We played in the yard. He slept in my room. What a great weekend! Homer was my dream dog.

We left Homer in the car.

Then, we heard a man yelling at a dog.

We heard a thump and a yelp.

"He's hitting a dog, Dad."

We walked in. The man saw us.

He looked very guilty.

"We need to talk," said Dad, "about Homer."

"Come into my office," the man said. I knew the smell.

He smelled of aftershave. I knew the smell.

"We can't keep Homer," said Dad.

On the man's desk was a bottle of aftershave. It was the same as my Dad's.

(Page 80)

(Page 81)

Then, came Monday, Dad came home from work. Homer and I were watching TV.

"Hey, Homer," Dad smiled and went to pet him.

I felt Homer change. He growled. The hair on his back stood up.

"Homer, what's up?" Dad said. But, Dad was scared. So was I.

Homer flew at Dad. He tried to bite him. Dad's jacket was thick. So, he wasn't hurt.

Dad left the room. Homer was shaking. He sat close to me. Dad opened the door. Homer changed again. He snarled and barked. Dad stayed away from Homer the rest of the night.

It was the same on Tuesday. We put Homer out in the yard.

"I can't take much more of this," Dad said.

On Wednesday, Homer bit Dad. He had to have stitches. Dad said that Homer had to go. I cried.

The next weekend, on Saturday, we drove to Animal Rescue. Homer didn't bark at Dad.

I begged, "Please, can we keep him, Dad? He's OK now."

Dad held up his hurt hand. "No, son."

(Page 82)

Directions: Think about the story you have read.
Draw a line from the sentence to its matching picture.

1. The boy and his dad went to Animal Rescue to get a dog.

2. Homer growled at Dad.

3. Homer bit Dad on the hand.

4. Dad said that Homer had to go back to Animal Rescue.

5. The smell of aftershave was the problem. The mean man and Dad smelled the same.

Directions: Antonyms are two different words that have the opposite meaning. For example, "hot" and "cold" are antonyms. Draw a line from each word in **Column A** to its matching antonym in **Column B**.

<u>Column A</u>   <u>Column B</u>

happy   **far**

mean   **little**

long   **sad**

near   **quiet**

loud   **nice**

big   **short**

Directions: Write an answer to the following question.   *Drawing Conclusions*

What do you think will happen to the man who was so mean to the dogs?

_____

_ _

_____

_ _

_____

_ _

_____

_ _

_____

_ _

_____

Fill in the blanks. Use the Word Bank.

Word Bank: asleep fairy float friends hair long one play Raify Sandy tapped

1. Carrie's best friend was named _____.

2. The girls were _____ for only _____ year.

3. Carrie's dog was named _____.

4. Raify had _____ white _____.

5. Raify _____ Sandy's nose, and he fell _____.

6. Raify almost seemed to _____.

7. One day, Raify said, "I can't _____ with you anymore."

8. Sandy looked like he had _____ dust on his nose.

Let's draw a conclusion!

On another sheet of paper, answer these questions. What was Raify? At the end of the story, why did Sandy jump around and bark?

(Page 85)

A SCARY STORY

Fiction Story 11

Raify

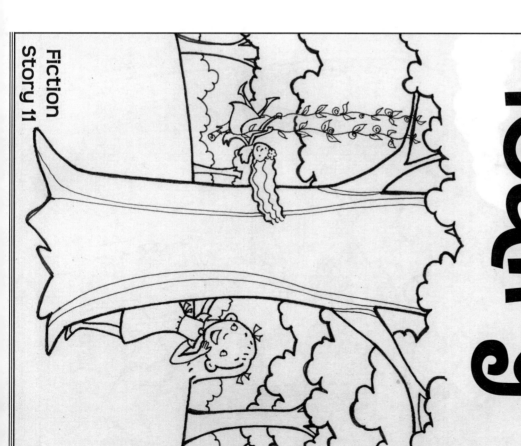

The next day, Sandy and I were in the woods. He barked. He jumped up and down. He wagged his tail. It looked like he was playing.

"Raify?" I called. Nothing. She didn't answer me.

When we got home, Mom looked at Sandy.

"What's that on his nose?" she asked. I looked. His nose sparkled.

"Why Sandy, you look like you have fairy dust on your nose," she laughed.

(Page 86)

(Page 87)

Raify

When I was small, I had a best friend. Oh, how I loved her. She was tiny and very pretty. Her hair was white and very long. Her name was Raify. We were friends for one year.

There were woods at the back of our house. The day I met Raify, I was walking in the woods with our dog, Sandy.

It was summer. It was a hot day. But, it felt cool in the woods.

I knew Raify liked me, but she never let me touch her. Once, I put my hand on her back.

She moved away and said, "Don't touch me!"

I was shocked. I'd felt something weird under her coat! There were two lumps on her back.

"Don't you go to school?" I asked her.

"My people don't. We don't need to."

One day, Raify was sad. When we said goodbye, she cried. "Carrie, I can't play with you anymore. I only had one year to play with you. Now, it's over."

Then, she said something strange. "You won't see me anymore. But, I'll see you."

(Page 88)

(Page 89)

"Hello," said a voice. I jumped. There was no one there. Sandy stopped walking. He seemed scared too.

Then, out she came from behind a tree. She wore a white dress and a white jacket. Her hair sparkled. She was like a lightbulb in the dark woods.

"My name's Raify," she said. Sandy barked and he shook.

I told her my name. "Hi, I'm Carrie."

Raify put her hand out to him. She tapped him on the nose. Then, he just fell asleep. Sandy had never fallen asleep in the woods before!

Raify was odd, but I liked her.

I liked her green, green eyes. I liked her white, lacy dress. I liked the way she smiled at me. She was so light on her feet. She almost seemed to float!

After that, we met every day after school. She asked me about lots of things. She asked me about school. She asked me about my home. She didn't know much. She didn't even know what a TV was!

KE-804090 © Key Education–*Trendy Topics: Scary Stories – Raify*

(Page 90)

KE-804090 © Key Education–*Trendy Topics: Scary Stories – Raify*

Name _____

Directions: Choose a word from the Word Bank to answer each crossword question. Write the answer in the correct word boxes.

Word Bank

Carrie   fairy

nose   Raify   said

Sandy   see

DOWN

2. Carrie's tiny friend was called _____.

5. Something sparkled on Sandy's _____.

ACROSS

1. Raify was a _____.

3. Raify met the girl, _____, in the woods.

4. _____ was Carrie's dog.

6. Raify _____,"I only had one year to play with you."

7. Carrie's mom could _____ fairy dust on Sandy's nose.

Name

Directions: Write an answer to the following question. *Drawing Conclusions*

Why do you think Raify could only play for a year?

Directions: Here is a picture from the story. Follow the directions.

1. Color Carrie's dress blue.

2. Color Sandy brown.

3. Color Carrie's shoes and hair bows pink.

4. Draw some small stars around Raify.

5. Draw and color something on the grass for the girls and Sandy to play with.

6. Color the grass and leaves on the trees green.

7. Color the tree trunks brown.

Fill in the blanks. Use the Word Bank.

Word Bank: city   country   ghost   gone
hospital   house   living   mom   notes   out
tic-tac-toe   uncle   wall   words

1. The _____ lived in the _____.

2. The boy was used to _____ in the _____.

3. The boy's _____ was in the _____.

4. The boy saw _____ on the wall.

5. The words said, "Get _____. This is my _____."

6. In the morning, the words were _____.

7. The _____ wrote nasty _____ on the _____.

8. Now, the ghost and the uncle play _____.

Let's draw a conclusion!

On another sheet of paper, write a story about why you think the ghost still lives in the house. And, why does it write on the wall?

A SCARY STORY

Words on a Wall

Fiction Story 12

Mom came home three days later. I was so happy to leave that house!

At Christmas, Mom sent my uncle a card. I put a letter in with it.

"Do you still get nasty notes from that ghost?"

He wrote back:

"I get notes, but not nasty ones. Last week, I wrote on the wall too. I wrote, 'Let's be friends. There's room in the house for both of us.'"

"Last night, we played tic-tac-toe on the wall. Why don't you come and visit? You could play with us."

"Thanks, but no thanks," I wrote back.

(Page 94)

(Page 95)

Words on a Wall

It was a long time ago. I was only 10 years old. But, I still dream about it.

I still wake up with the shakes.

I still sleep with the light on.

Me, a 30-year-old man and I still sleep with the light on!

This is what happened 20 years ago.

My mom was in the hospital. I had to stay with my uncle. I didn't like him. And, he didn't like me. Yet, there was no place else for me to go.

My uncle put toast on my plate.
He said, "Looks like you didn't sleep
too good."

I just stared back at him.

He sat down and said, "Don't tell me.
You had a pen pal visit."

"Yes!" I said.

"Let me guess. Did it say get out or go
home—something like that?"

"Yes!" I said.

"It never gives up." My uncle took a
sip of coffee.

"What never gives up?" I asked.

My uncle said, "I didn't believe in
ghosts. But, I do now. It never hurts
anyone. It just leaves nasty notes."

(Page 96)

KE-804090 © Key Education–Trendy Topics: Scary Stories – Words on a Wall

KE-804090 © Key Education–Trendy Topics: Scary Stories – Words on a Wall

(Page 97)

He lived in the country. I was used to living in the city. I grew up with lights and noise. At my uncle's house, there was only silence at night. Silence, like a buzz, deep in my head.

I missed my mom. I worried about her. What if she didn't get better? What if I had to always live here?

It was hard for me to sleep. I would just stare at the wall in front of me.

Then, it started. I saw a black line on the wall. The line was shiny, like wet paint. The line became the letter G. Next, a new line became an E. Then, a letter T. Soon, there were huge words on the wall. Black drips from the letters rolled down to the floor. On the wall I read:

GET OUT
THIS IS MY HOUSE!

I wanted to get out! But, the words on the wall were next to the door. I was too scared to move. I put my head under the sheets. I stayed there.

I must have gone to sleep. I woke up when the sun lit up the room. The words were gone. The wall was clean and white.

(Page 98)

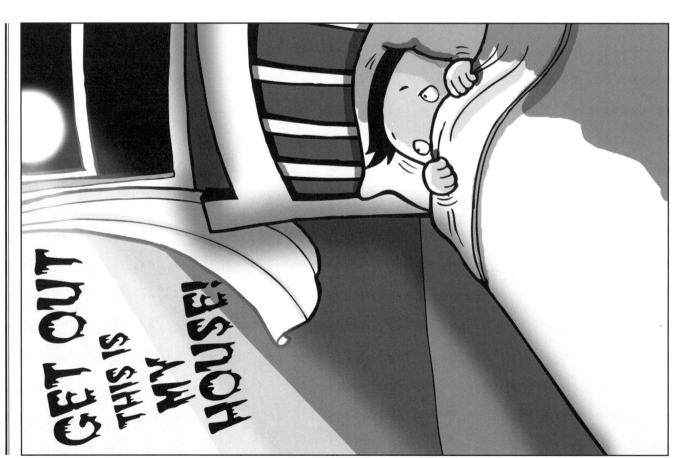

Directions: Read the question in each box. Write your answer in each speech bubble.

1. What do you think the boy is thinking?

2. What do you think the boy is thinking now?

3. What do you think the uncle is saying to the boy?

4. What do you think the uncle is thinking?

Name _____

Directions: Circle the words from the Word Bank in the word search. *Word Search*
The words may be horizontal or vertical.

Word Bank
city
country
drip
ghost
hospital
house
letters
room
sun
uncle
wall
words

d	h	q	j	k	d	b	w	u
c	o	u	n	t	r	y	o	n
t	s	u	n	t	i	r	r	c
s	p	o	p	g	p	o	d	l
c	i	t	y	h	o	u	s	e
c	t	r	o	o	m	m	o	g
e	a	m	a	s	w	a	l	l
c	l	e	t	t	e	r	s	r

Directions: Circle **yes** or **no** for each sentence. *Reading for Details*

1. The boy's mom was in the hospital. **yes** **no**

2. The boy was from the city. **yes** **no**

3. The uncle lived in the country. **yes** **no**

4. The boy liked staying at his uncle's house. **yes** **no**

5. The boy liked the happy words he saw on the wall. **yes** **no**

6. The uncle played tic-tac-toe with the ghost. **yes** **no**

Fill in the blanks. Use the Word Bank.

Word Bank: better boy dare fell Gary
graveyard run scared tripped yellow

1. The boys wanted to ——— around
   the graveyard.

2. ——————— liked to do scary things.

3. The boy ——— over a tree root
   and ——— down.

4. He was too ——— to move.

5. Then, he saw a ——— glowing
   light and felt ———.

6. The yellow light spoke and sounded like a
   ———.

7. The boy ran out of the ———.

8. Gary doesn't ——— anyone
   anymore.

Let's draw a conclusion!

On another sheet of paper, answer this question.
Why do you think the glowing ghost helped the
boy get out of the graveyard?

(Page 101)

A SCARY STORY

Fiction Story 13

Gary looked at me. He patted my arms and my head.

"What are you doing?" I said.

"You're glowing!" he said.

I looked. He was right. My body had a halo!

"I think I've just seen a ghost," I told him.

"Let's get out of here! You can tell me all about it at home," said Gary.

"What about the dare?" I asked. You have to go into the graveyard now."

"No way!" said Gary.

Gary doesn't dare anyone anymore!

(Page 102)

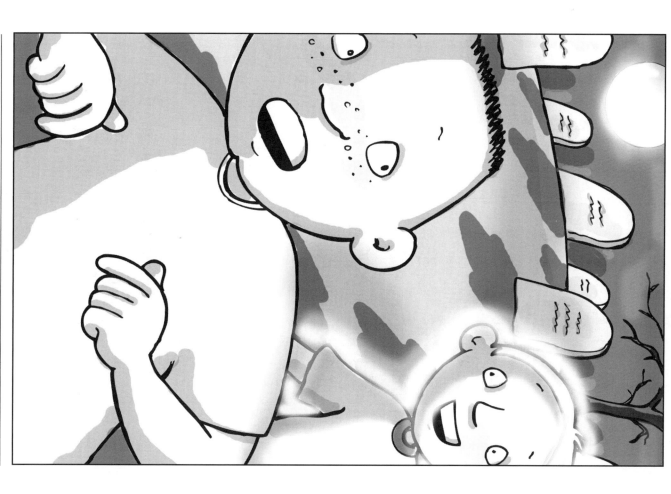

(Page 103)

The Graveyard

It was dark. It was cold. I was lost. There was blood on my knee. I was in the graveyard all by myself.

And, late at night," Gary had said. "We have to walk around the graveyard — all on our own!

Gary was my friend. He liked doing scary stuff. I didn't, but I liked Gary. That's how I came to be in this awful mess. I had to go into the graveyard first. Gary would go in when I came out.

"Back so soon!" It was Gary, making one of his jokes.

"Sorry," I said. "Were you cold?" I didn't want to tell him about the boy. He'd just laugh at me.

"What do you mean?" Gary said. "You only just left. You couldn't have run all the way around the graveyard."

"I did. I've been gone a long, long time," I said.

"Look!" Gary said, and he showed me his watch. It was 10:00. I went into the graveyard at 10:00! How could it still be 10:00?

(Page 104)

(Page 105)

I ran halfway around the graveyard.

Then, I tripped over a tree root. I fell on the ground. My knee was cut. When I got up, I didn't know which way to go.

I felt panic in my chest. My leg hurt. I was too scared to move.

That's when I felt the change. The air was warm. There was a soft light— a yellow glow. I didn't know what it was. It felt good so I wasn't scared.

"It's OK," said a voice.

The voice was kind. It came from the light.

"I'll show you how to get out of here."

It was a boy's voice.

The light moved. In the light, I could see a boy. He was hidden in the light most of the time. Every so often I could see his arm, his foot, or his head. I walked behind him. I felt safe and happy.

I saw the gate. The light faded. The boy was gone.

(Page 106)

Name

Directions: Read the sentences at the bottom of the page.
Cut out each sentence and glue it under its matching picture.

Gary said, "You're glowing!"

There was a soft glowing light.

It was 10:00! How could it still be 10:00?

Gary and I were going to run around the graveyard.

Creative Writing

Directions: Pretend you are a reporter for a newspaper.
What two questions would you ask the glowing light?

1.

2.

Directions: Read each question. Circle the correct answer.

Reading for Details

1. After the boy fell, what did he see?

nothing　　　　**a glowing light**　　　　**his friend Gary**

2. How did the light make the boy feel?

good　　　　**scared**　　　　**mad**

3. What did Gary like to do?

eat hotdogs　　　　**tell time**　　　　**dare people**

Fill in the blanks. Use the Word Bank.

Word Bank: brownies   chip   clean   cookie   floor   gone   honey   jobs   walk

1. Nana would put _____ on the _____.

2. The chocolate _____ cookies were burned.

3. The _____ sheet was black.

4. _____ are kind of like elves.

5. Brownies like to do _____ that people don't like to do.

6. Nana and her granddaughter went for a _____.

7. When they got home, the cookie sheet was _____.

8. And, the honey was _____.

Let's draw a conclusion!

On another sheet of paper, make a list of the jobs that you would like brownies to do for you.

(Page 109)

A SCARY STORY

Fiction Story 14

Honey on the Floor

When we got back, I went into the kitchen. Nana was still in the hall. I saw the cookie sheet. It was still on the table, but it was clear! I ran to the corner of the kitchen. I put my finger in the corner. No honey! The honey was gone!

Nana came in. She picked up the cookie sheet and looked at me. Then, she winked and put the cookie sheet away. She didn't say a word about how clean it was. The smile on her face said it all.

(Page 110)

(Page 111)

Honey on the Floor

My Nana had some funny ideas. She used to dab honey on the kitchen floor.

My mom didn't like it. She'd say, "You'll get ants."

"You grew up in this house," Nana said to my mom. "Have you ever seen ants in here?"

"No," said my mom. "But still, you shouldn't put honey on the floor."

"I don't tell you what to do. Don't you tell me what to do," said Nana.

Nana was cross. So, Mom kept quiet after that.

She said, "Brownies are like elves.

You leave honey out for them.

Then, they might do a job for you.

A job that you don't like to do."

I didn't ask Nana any more questions.

Maybe she was a little bit crazy.

"Let's go out for a walk," Nana said.

She left the burned cookie sheet on the table. She said that she would wash it when we got back from our walk.

(Page 112)

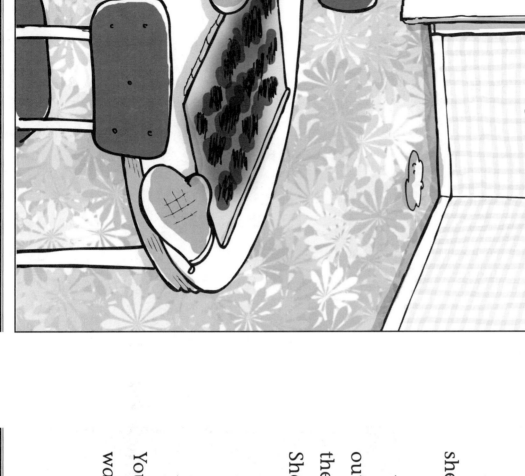

(Page 113)

Once when I was staying with my Nana, we made cookies. The cookies had burned, and the cookie sheet was ruined. It was all black.

"Oh, I hate washing burned cookie sheets," said Nana.

Then, she went to the shelf and took out the pot of honey. She walked to the corner of the room and bent down. She put a dab of honey on the floor.

"Nana, why do you do that?" I asked.

Nana said, "I don't want to tell you. Your mother thinks I'm crazy. I don't want you to think the same thing."

"Oh, Nana, I won't! Please tell me."

Nana looked at me for a long time. Then, she said, "What do you know about brownies?"

"I like them best when they're still warm!" I said and rubbed my tummy.

"Not that kind of brownie. Real brownies. The ones that are kind of like elves. They like to do jobs for people."

I giggled.

"You see, you do think I'm crazy." Nana looked cross.

I said I was sorry and gave her a hug. I asked her to tell me more. At first, she said no, but I begged her.

(Page 114)

KE-804090 © Key Education –Trendy Topics: Scary Stories – Honey on the Floor

KE-804090 © Key Education –Trendy Topics: Scary Stories – Honey on the Floor

Directions: Look at the pictures at the bottom of the page.
Cut them out along the dotted lines and glue them in the correct order.

1	2	3

Name _____

Directions: A **fact** is something that is true. An **opinion** is something that a person thinks, believes, or feels. Write the word "**fact**" or the word "**opinion**" next to each sentence.

_____   1.   Nana had some funny ideas.

_____   2.   Nana would put honey on the floor.

_____   3.   Nana and the little girl went for a walk.

_____   4.   Maybe Nana is a little crazy.

_____   5.   Nana and the little girl burned the cookies.

_____   6.   After the walk, the cookie sheet was clean.

Directions: Draw and color what you think a brownie looks like.   *Creative Art*

(Page 117)

MY OWN STORY

(Page 118)

(Page 119)

(Page 120)

(Page 121)

(Page 122)

New Vocabulary to Be Introduced Prior to Reading Each Story

Story 1 – Bella's Photo
- camera
- contest
- fullback
- hooves
- Kenya
- photos
- safari
- speech
- throats
- vacation

Story 2 – The Flying Carpet
- carpet
- hungry
- magic
- musty
- special

Story 3 – Message in a Bottle
- arrested
- beach
- bottle
- daughter
- hero
- Hilary
- message
- officer
- sunglasses
- thief
- ugly

Story 4 – Never Again!
- bottom
- growled
- heard
- scared
- skiier
- skiing
- slope

Story 5 – On Thin Ice
- afraid
- brave
- crack
- Michigan
- numb
- Texas

Story 6 – The Haunted Classroom
- classroom
- ghost
- guilty
- haunted
- wrong

Story 7 – The Ring
- birthday
- eighteen
- noise
- shaking
- slipper
- tiptoed
- tomorrow

Story 8 –The Lady of the Lake
- cabin
- cousins
- haunted
- idiot
- Phil
- quiet
- shore
- shout
- stupid
- towards

Story 9 – Sick Brother
- blood
- brother
- grinned
- mayo
- mouth
- pickles
- popsicles
- worried

Story 10 – Homer
- aftershave
- guilty
- Homer
- rescue
- tomorrow
- watching

Story 11 – Raify
- Carrie
- fairy
- Raify
- Sandy
- sparkled
- strange

Story 12 – Words on a Wall
- believe
- country
- hospital
- huge
- leave
- tic-tac-toe
- uncle

Story 13 – The Graveyard
- dare
- Gary
- ghost
- glowing
- graveyard
- knee
- voice

Story 14 – Honey on the Floor
- brownies
- corner
- elves
- floor
- honey
- kitchen
- Nana
- questions
- ruined

Answer Key

ADVENTURE STORIES

Story 1
Bella's Photo
Booklet page 12 (page 5):
1. David
2. small
3. Kenya
4. zebras
5. tents
6. gone
7. picked
8. photo

Page 11

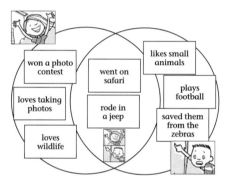

Page 12 (Top)

e	l	e	p	h	a	n	t	s
b	n	t	h	o	n	z	y	a
t	K	h	o	j	e	e	p	f
t	e	n	t	s	l	b	n	a
u	n	r	o	e	i	r	l	r
c	y	s	s	e	o	a	o	i
D	a	v	i	d	n	s	v	j
w	i	l	d	B	e	l	l	a

Page 12 (Bottom)
1. T, 2. T, 3. F, 4. T, 5. F, 6. T

Story 2
The Flying Carpet
Booklet page 12 (page 13):
1. carpet
2. smell
3. magic
4. sit, flower

5. room
6. beach, camels
7. men
8. stone

Page 19
Check students' work

Page 20 (Top)
1. c.,   2. a.,   3. d.,   4. b.

Page 20 (Bottom)
Check students' work

Story 3
Message in a Bottle
Booklet page 12 (page 21):
1. sleep, read
2. glass
3. bottle, baby
4. black
5. message
6. grab
7. police
8. arrested

Page 27 –

Page 28 (Top)
Check students' work

Page 28 (Bottom)
1. yes,   2. no,   3. yes,   4. no,
5. no,   6. no,   7. yes

Story 4
Never Again!
Booklet page 12 (page 29):
1. Marc
2. not
3. good
4. stop
5. growl, bear
6. fast
7. Slow
8. crashed, snow

Page 35

Page 36 (Top)
Check students' work

Page 36 (Bottom)
2. One bad ski experience and I will never ski again!

Story 5
On Thin Ice
Booklet page 12 (page 37):
1. Cal
2. snow, ice
3. skate
4. Paul
5. crack
6. cold
7. Help, help
8. man, sled

Page 43
Check students' work

Page 44 (Top)
Check students' work

Page 44 (Bottom)
1. c.,   2. d.,   3. a.,   4. b.

MYSTERIES

Story 6
The Haunted Classroom
Booklet page 12 (page 45):
1. field, zoo
2. Toby
3. money
4. washed, walked
5. Mrs. Green
6. book
7. ghost
8. mouse, eating

Page 51
Check students' work

Page 52 (Top)
1. the zoo,   2. dog,   3. car,
4. mouse

Page 52 (Bottom)
Check students' work

Story 7
The Ring
Booklet page 12 (page 53):
1. grandma
2. loved, ring
3. pillow
4. tiptoed, table
5. slipper
6. water
7. never
8. give, birthday

Page 59

Page 60 (Top)
Check students' work

Page 60 (Bottom)
1. T, 2. T, 3. F, 4. F, 5. T, 6. T

Story 8
The Lady of the Lake
Booklet page 12 (page 61):
1. Lady, Lake
2. sit, quiet
3. white
4. walk
5. ghost
6. friends
7. sandbar
8. aunt

Page 67
Check students' work

Page 68 (Top)
1. on the shore of a lake
2. sit and be quiet
3. the aunt

Page 68 (Bottom)
Check students' work

Story 9
Sick Brother
Booklet page 12 (page 69):
1. liked, doctor
2. popsicles
3. legs, blue
4. jeans
5. week
6. mayo, pickles
7. sick
8. buy

Page 75
Check students' work

Page 76 (Top)
Check students' work

Page 76 (Bottom)
1. fact,   2. opinion,   3. fact,
4. fact,   5. opinion,   6. fact

Story 10
Homer
Booklet page 12 (page 77):
1. Animal, dog
2. Homer
3. long, black
4. dream
5. bite
6. back
7. hitting
8. smelled

Page 83
1. c.,   2. e.,   3. a.,
4. b.,   5. d.

Page 84 (Top)
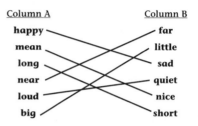

Page 84 (Bottom)
Check students' work

SCARY STORIES

Story 11
Raify
Booklet page 12 (page 85):
1. Raify
2. friends, one
3. dog, Sandy
4. long, hair
5. tapped, asleep
6. float
7. play
8. fairy

Page 91

f	a	i	r	y
		a		
C	a	r	r	i	e
		f		
S	a	n	d	y
		o		
		s	a	i	d
s	e	e		

Page 92 (Top)
Check students' work

Page 92 (Bottom)
Check students' work

Story 12
Words on a Wall
Booklet page 12 (page 93):
1. uncle, country
2. living, city
3. mom, hospital
4. words
5. out, house
6. gone
7. ghost, notes, wall
8. tic-tac-toe

Page 99
Check students' work

Page 100 (Top)

d	h	q	j	k	d	b	w	u
c	o	u	n	t	r	y	o	n
t	s	u	n	t	i	r	r	c
s	p	o	p	g	p	o	d	l
c	i	t	y	h	o	u	s	e
c	t	r	o	o	m	m	o	g
e	a	m	a	s	w	a	l	l
c	l	e	t	t	e	r	s	r

Page 100 (Bottom)
1. yes, 2. yes, 3. yes, 4. no, 5. no, 6. yes

Story 13
The Graveyard
Booklet page 12 (page 101):
1. run
2. Gary
3. tripped, fell
4. scared
5. yellow, better
6. boy
7. graveyard
8. dare

Page 107

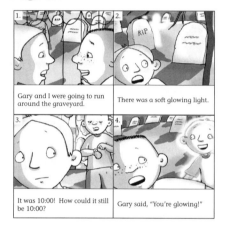

Page 108 (Top)
Check students' work

Page 108 (Bottom)
1. a glowing light
2. good
3. dare people

Story 14
Honey on the Floor
Booklet page 12 (page 109):
1. honey, floor
2. chip
3. cookie
4. Brownies
5. jobs
6. walk
7. clean
8. gone

Page 115 –

Page 116 (Top)
1. opinion, 2. fact, 3. fact,
4. opinion, 5. fact, 6. fact

Page 116 (Bottom)
Check students' work

Correlations to the Standards

This book supports the NCTE/IRA *Standards for the English Language Arts.*

Each activity in this book supports one or more of the following standards:

1. **Students read many different types of print and nonprint texts for a variety of purposes.** *Trendy Topics: Fiction* includes fifteen reading passages at varying reading levels, along with audio recordings of those passages to build both reading and listening skills. It also includes comprehension activities that require students to read and interpret images.

2. **Students use a variety of strategies to build meaning while reading.** Comprehension activities focusing on drawing conclusions, main idea, classification, cause and effect, reading for details, sequencing, inference, and vocabulary, among other skills, support this standard.

3. **Students communicate in spoken, written, and visual form, for a variety of purposes and a variety of audiences.** Activities in *Trendy Topics: Fiction* incorporate drawing and writing for a variety of purposes and audiences.

4. **Students use the writing process to write for different purposes and different audiences.** *Trendy Topics: Fiction* includes writing activities focused on a variety of audiences and purposes.

5. **Students incorporate knowledge of language conventions (grammar, spelling, punctuation), media techniques, and genre to create and discuss a variety of print and nonprint texts.** Writing activities in *Trendy Topics: Fiction* take different forms, such as sentences, lists, stories, and interview questions, allowing students to practice different forms of writing and writing conventions.

6. **Students use spoken, written, and visual language for their own purposes, such as to learn, for enjoyment, or to share information.** The engaging stories in *Trendy Topics: Fiction* will motivate students to read independently and the skill-building activities will support students in becoming more effective independent readers and writers.

How to Download CD— Audio and PDF Files

To play the Audio stories in a CD Player

Place the CD in a CD player and play the CD as you would any audio or music CD. The pdf files on the CD will not appear or interfere with the audio stories.

Download the CD into a Windows PC

Put the enhanced CD in your computer CD drive and go to "My Computers." Double click on the CD icon where it says "TT_Fiction" in order to play the audio stories. To view and print the pdf files, right click on the CD icon and select "Open." Then, all the pdf files will appear. Click to open a file and then print.

Download the CD into an Apple/Macintosh Computer

Put the enhanced CD into the VCD drive. Two pictures of the CD will appear on the desktop. (See figure 1.) Click on the CD labeled "Audio CD" and the storybook soundtracks will download to itunes. Use itunes to play each story from your Apple computer.

figure 1.

Click on the CD labled "TT_Fiction" and a folder will appear, labeled "KE-804090- Storybook Storybook & Activity PDFs." (See figure 2.) Click on this folder and it will open to show you all the PDFs of the Storybooks and Activity Pages. (See figure 3.)

figure 2.

KE-804090-Storybook & Activity PDFs

Click on the PDF of your choice and then print.

Story 1–Activity Page 11.pdf
Story 1–Activity Page 12.pdf
Story 2–Activity Page 19.pdf
Story 2–Activity Page 20.pdf
Story 3–Activity Page 27.pdf
Story 3–Activity Page 28.pdf
Story 4–Activity Page 35.pdf
Story 4–Activity Page 36.pdf
Story 5–Activity Page 43.pdf
Story 5–Activity Page 44.pdf
Story 6–Activity Page 51.pdf
Story 6–Activity Page 52.pdf
Story 7–Activity Page 59.pdf
Story 7–Activity Page 60.pdf
Story 8–Activity Page 67.pdf
Story 8–Activity Page 68.pdf
Story 9–Activity Page 75.pdf
Story 9–Activity Page 76.pdf
Story 10–Activity Page 83.pdf
Story 10–Activity Page 84.pdf
Story 11–Activity Page 91.pdf
Story 11–Activity Page 92.pdf
Story 12–Activity Page 99.pdf
Story 12–Activity Page 100.pdf
Story 13–Activity Page 107.pdf
Story 13–Activity Page 108.pdf
Story 14–Activity Page 115.pdf
Story 14–Activity Page 116.pdf
Storybook 1–Bella's Photo Pages 5–10.pdf
Storybook 2–The Flying Carpet Pages 13–18.pdf
Storybook 3–Message in a Bottle Pages 21–26.pdf
Storybook 4–Never Again! Pages 29–34.pdf
Storybook 5–On Thin Ice Pages 37–42.pdf
Storybook 6–The Haunted Classroom Pages 45–50.pdf
Storybook 7–The Ring Pages 53–58.pdf
Storybook 8–The Lady of the Lake Pages 61–66.pdf
Storybook 9–Sick Brother Pages 69–74.pdf
Storybook 10–Homer Pages 77–82.pdf
Storybook 11–Raify Pages 85–90.pdf
Storybook 12–Words on a Wall Pages 93–98.pdf
Storybook 13–The Graveyard Pages 101–106.pdf
Storybook 14–Honey on the Floor Pages 109–114.pdf

figure 3.

(This is what the list of PDFs will look like on PCs and Apple computers.)